Needs new barcode
Sticker - won't
read.

For Jenny, fleetingly known, yet always remembered
and for Zoë Silver, a golden friend – H.R.

For John – A.L.

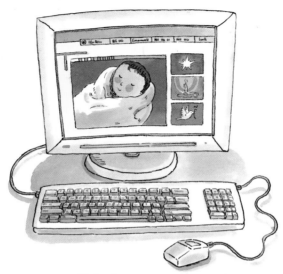

The sale of this book will help to support the work of SANDS –
Stillbirth and Neonatal Death Society.

E-MAIL: JESUS@BETHLEHEM
by Hilary Robinson and Anthony Lewis

British Library Cataloguing in Publication Data
A catalogue record of this book is available
from the British Library.

ISBN: 0340 88463 0 (PB)

2 4 6 8 10 9 7 5 3

Text copyright © Hilary Robinson 1999
Illustrations copyright © Anthony Lewis 1999

The right of Hilary Robinson to be identified as the author
and Anthony Lewis as the illustrator of this Work
has been asserted by them in accordance with the
Copyright, Designs and Patents Act 1988.

First published in Great Britain by Macdonald Young Books.
This edition published 2004 by Hodder Children's Books
An imprint of Hodder Headline Limited
338 Euston Road
London NW1 3BH

Printed in China

e-mail: Jesus@Bethlehem

Hilary Robinson   Anthony Lewis

Hodder
Children's
Books

A division of Hodder Headline Limited

Let's imagine that Jesus was born today.

The shepherds hear the good news...

on their mobile phones.

Then, hot off the printing press...

Later, on television, everyone sees a newsflash.

And, via a satellite in the night sky,
the three kings hear the news.

The shepherds flock to the scene.

The kings travel by private jet.

They bring gifts of gold,

frankincense

and myrrh.

And are stopped at Customs.

Then news spreads on the World Wide Web that a great teacher has been born on Earth.

And e-mails are sent from nation to nation.

And every country sings out to the sound of

the Band of Angels with their new big hit...

And Jesus becomes a new star
in many people's lives.

Yet, it's about two thousand years since Jesus was born. There have been lots of changes. But everything Jesus taught and gave us then still lives on today.